© Matthew Caley

The Scene Of My Former Triumph

© All copyrights remain with the author

First Edition

ISBN 1-903110-29-7

Cover Design by
Owen Benwell

**Published in 2005 by
Wrecking Ball Press**
24 CAVENDISH SQUARE • HULL • ENGLAND • HU3 1SS

The Scene Of My Former Triumph

Matthew Caley

Wrecking Ball Press

Acknowledgements

Are due to the editors of the following magazines, periodicals, publications and websites where these poems, or versions of them, first appeared:

Billy Liar, Dog, Fat City Anthology, The Independent, The Independent On Sunday, Limelight 8, www.thepoem.co.uk, Magma, Poetry Review, The Rat's Mirror, TLS, The Tabla Book Of New Verse, The Wolf no 10.

ABBA CD recieved Special Mention in the TLS/Blackwells Competition 2003; *Low Maintenance Roof-Garden* won Third Prize in The National Poetry Competition 2002; *Three Is Just A Better Form Of Two* was Commended in The National Poetry Competition 2001; *Lines Written On A Prophylactic Found In A Brixton Gutter* was Commended in the Poetry London Competition 2000; part of *'Three Avatars'* - *The Wellspring*, recieved Special Mention in the TLS/Blackwells Competition 2001;

The Measurement Of Quims was published in a group chapbook from Ha'penny Press.

Just Passing Through was originally written for a collaborative exhibition with artist Stephen Nicholas in the Huisproject series in Tilberg, Holland, curated by Corrina Diepens and Ad Van Campenhout and was also published as *'X-Ray Haiku'* in The Dover Book Of Haiku. *The Family* was also originally written for a Caley/Nicholas collaboration.

Many thanks to Mr John Stammers and Mr Tim Cumming - the former for help, advice and the gift of a tapir; the latter for advocacy with discretion. To all those at The Poetry Society for a residency during the time this book was written.

For Pavla

and i.m J.D.H
1916-2003

'And an elegant internee sensed godlier litanies
In gangrened slattern lotteries in Laredo'
    ANTIC QUATRAINS. *Jackson Mac Low*

W.W.BEAUCHAMP: 'I'm not, look... I don't have a gun... I've never had a gun. I write. I'm a writer...'

WILLIAM MUNNEY: 'Writer?'

W.W.BEAUCHAMP: 'Yes.'

WILLIAM MUNNEY: 'What, letters and such?'

W.W.BEAUCHAMP: 'No, books'.

WILLIAM MUNNEY: 'Books?'

    from UNFORGIVEN. *Directed by Clint Eastwood 1992*

'I could've been Raskolnikov
But Mother Nature ripped me off"
    from MAGAZINE L.P 'THE CORRECT USE OF SOAP'
    Howard Devoto

'Tour well the slag-heaps, Royalty!'
    PART OF MANDEVILLE'S TRAVELS. *William Empson*

contents

Pledge	13
from The Mould Canticles	14
Lines Written Upon A Prophylactic Found In A Brixton Gutter	18
Moldy's Reliance	19
ABBA CD	20
Pantomime Horse	21
The Late Great Townes Van Zant	23
Three Is Just A Better Form Of Two	25
Towards A Philosophy Of Speed	27
The Fabulists	28
Of Books And Their Vicissitudes	30
The Novel	33
The Plot	35
The Smell Of Books	36
Ammonius Saccas	38
Is This Isthmus A Land-Mass Or Is This Land-Mass An Isthmus?	40
Ode : *Rapid Eye Movement*	42
Wallace Stevens At The Oboe	44
Birds And Their Shadows	49
The Measurement Of Quims	51
The Family	52

contents

Of Love And Its Vicissitudes	55
Sleepwalking For Beginners	57
Flight	59
Low Maintenance Roof Garden	60
Artic Fleece	62
Two Silver Birches	64
The Scene Of My Former Triumph	66
Remembering The Ilex Tree	69
Horse Longtitudes	71
Just Passing Through	72
Welcome To_____, Twinned With_____	75
Three Avatars	76
Serendipity Ode	78
Cul-De-Sac	82
The Critics Who Failed To Define Their Own Epoch	83
Tall Iced De-Caffeinated Latte	87
King-Size Rizlas	89
Barbary Ape	90
St Elsewhere	92
Big Sur	94
Indolent Beach Bum	95
Acupuncture	98

Pledge

Drugs. Alcohol. Little sister. And not necessarily by Trakl.
Such is my life. Thus I get by.
Even with this luminous canker on my wedding-tackle.
Yet if she would only pledge herself to me entirely,

I would willingly give up the bawds and the Bacchanalia,
get a sinecure, grow, eat an avocado and die.

from The Mould Canticles

Hamlet cawed The Soup Dragons decidedly off-key
above me in the wedge-shaped squat
its fan-tailed
over-run garden brambling out
to the railway bridge where an urban fox
slunk to an unseen culvert. *I'm free
to do what I want any old time* ran the lyrics

running in rainy rivulets down to me
in the dust-stippled room
in the shape of a thre'penny bit
hammering out narked sonnets on bottled *Stella*.
The kitchen stairs were flaked
with blistering paint, weeping faucets
mushrooms dewlapped with ugly petals of mould

but the backdoor steps were our vine-arbor and balcony
with a view of a thorn-spiked entanglement
hiding an ornamental pond
that Leigh and Vags
quite separately had fallen into
on more than one occasion
like drunken Alices

into the rabbit-hole. That famous day
when Hamlet returned from Brighton
replete with some slip of a thing
only to find his fraulein, Katia
still holed up
in his bed from the night before.
She flounced out with a certain am-dram flair

yelling -to the slip-
'I bet he still smells of me'.
Exactly at the same time a recent ex of mine
the bewitching Kira
smashed down the already smashed-in door
on account, or not, of an unpaid loan - £5.00-
and danced a jig in the rain

wounded as Frida Kahlo in her corset
and put a curse on the house.
Her words then seemed half-bestial, half-holy,
a mixture of slang and Sanskrit
plus the odd
goat-like grunt out of Alistair Crowley.
[Once we'd split -the deed was down to me -

Kira had excelled herself
by sinking an enlarged pig's heart
in a glass jar of formaldehyde, tied
with a silken, purple bow
and placing it on my doorstep for Valentine's Day. But
the sealing was uneven
and this ur-Hirst

burst and began to stink me out of hearth
and home. The selfsame former flat
I'd quickly emptied out
of every possible memory of J -
J who I still see clearly
striding the threadbare carpet at Lambert Road
for a guacamole nose-lick

from the fridge. See again the white glow
against her teak-dark body -
her *Tampax*-string a-swing
like a tiny, vestigial tail.
Diverting, briefly, here- if you peer at Courbet's *The Studio
                            Of The Painter,*
past the studious Dandy with his book
and slightly to the left, look

and you will see her, Miss Lemur,
paler, fainter,
indelible Jeanne Duvall, indelible]. Anyhow, Kira's violent curse
made Catherine cry, the first time I'd seen her cry
and also brought out Eva
our rent-a-Hariden 'earth-mother' next-door-neighbour
for a screaming duel

with Katia, now tense as a German verb
who then pissed off into the fractured black,
leaving Catherine, non-plussed, under-dressed
- the voluptuary
in *Dejeuner Sur l'Herb* -
on the doorstep softly murmuring 'Elm Street, Elm Street'.
Then it all went quiet. Kira, J, Frida, Alice, Stella

might never now come back
in the same disguise. And many
have slunk off into an unseen culvert.
All of us tenants of a block
so windy we felt like kites.
Even now I can still see
and describe - it's down to me -

the scene beneath the stairwell,
each paint-blister, mould-petal
hanging in the balance between earth and air.
Down to me to note
it as it all rots
from the inside yet sends me singing
slightly off-key, maybe

like The Soup Dragons sung by Hamlet up in his eyrie.

Lines Written Upon A Prophylactic Found In A Brixton Gutter

O useless balloon, supine, not the colour of dolor
but see-thru, salmon-pink, plugged with your load of ore
draped in the grating side by side
with imploded pizza-stars and half a crepe.

Squished jellyfish of desire, trodden under the fly-boy trainers
of crack-dealers by the Taxi-rank and noodle-bar
-witness to a union of souls or alleyway tremble -
spermicidal eel, you know the perfidious trade-routes,

how the underground waters of the Effra
distabilise our feet, how pomegranate or melon-seeds
from the glass-arcades stuck in the tread of our boots

might spring up a rash of fruit trees in the inner city
sometime and knowing also how joy is brief [and rarely
                    sanctioned by the Pontiff]
you dangle-drop, precariously, swim out for the open sea.

Moldy's Reliance

Egg and chips; ham, egg and chips; sausage egg and chips,
        coffee with two sugars
became his litany and creed, to love all he surveyed :
dogs, Rasta-adorned corners, Messers *Fuller, Moon & Fuller* who
        were, he swore,
a team of conveyancing agents and not a mid-period poem by
        Robert Graves.

Pass the sugar, mate- uggh??, oh, sure.

To suddenly became aware of - *le differance-*
between a quarter-moon and a sickle moon, between Soho, New York
and Soho Square, between Birmingham, Alabama and
Birmingham anywhere,

between a slim volume and a volume of thin air
-like *Squibs*, that notable rant against the Belgians written by
a syphilitic Charlie Baudelaire, who, on his final lecture tour

felt 'the flutter of imbecility' and longed for 'son mere'.
then petered out along with his elegant coat-cuffs and his hair.

-Sorry, again mate- pass the salt? -whaaat??, oh, sure.

ABBA CD

O verily you were readily forgot
until, spring-cleaning, I happened upon my 'best of' Abba CD,
became engulfed in the golden chords of *Knowing Me,
Knowing You,* as those resourceful Swedes, so apt and ageless at regret

played on, song after song, and suddenly your body-heat
was burned back into me. O Benny and Bjorn, hamster-faced Svengali's,
how your verse/chorus - middle-eight - verse/chorus excoriates me,
excoriates the delicate

membrane of avoidance, for when Agnetha, embodiment of
                              exultant melancho
-lia, stands back to back with the other one -the redhead-
[un]heroically rhyming 'Glasgow' with 'last show'

it raises your spectre back from the dead
trilling a supe-per-per, troup-per-per of Scandinavian brio
until you retreat down a secret track, in a white shift, etiolated.

Pantomime Horse

Captain Beefheart steps out at The Elk Lounge.
A wolf's-paw is hanging from his cummerbund.
Seattle rain consists of pain and grunge.
A feral grunt is hard to understand.

That wah-wah peddle meddles with the wave-band.
Captain Beefheart steps out at The Elk Lounge.
The A&R department hunt a wunderkind.
Seattle rain consists of pain and grunge.

Most sad songs are in the key of E
and middle-eights hard to negotiate.
Gram Parsons checks in at *The Joshua Tree*.
A tumbleweed blows down The Interstate.

A lucky drummer joins The Truly Great.
Most sad songs are in the key of E.
Morrisey and God claim to be celibate.
Gram Parsons checks out of *The Joshua Tree*.

If it's Tuesday then it must be Belgium
A lucky drummer joins The Truly Great.
Come in Whitney Houston we have a problem.
Morrisey and God claim to be celibate.

Chicago headline just above Roxette.
If it's Tuesday then it must be Belgium.
The once-obscure release a huge box-set.
Come in Whitney Houston we have a problem.

Some chart-topping Diva blows a fuse.
Chicago headline just above Roxette.
Lowdown & Dirty : Spice Girls Sing The Blues.
The once-obscure release a huge box-set.

Jim Morrison and Elvis live on Teeside.
Seattle rain consists of pain and grunge.
All our best songs crowded on the B-side
as Captain Beefheart steps out at The Elk Lounge.

The Late Great Townes Van Zant

Townes Van Zant
is divided into three.

One third's gone to Dido,
tombstoned under a cypress tree.

Another third's been scattered
off a Fort Worth balcony

like scorched or bleached confetti. The very next third is now
                              interred
in this Mason-jar on the mantlepiece behind me.

Townes Van Zant
is divided into three.

–

That airy cartwheel of tumbleweed
on a heat-haze free

-way might be another third. Another's being delivered
to Medicine Bow via Albequerque

by way of an improper pin-boy. Talent
is belligerent

and grinds the body to gruel. No fool
Townes Van Zant.

The modality of his yodel
like trying to lasso ghee.

—

Townes Van Zant
is divided into three.

The executives at Columbia
couldn't tell a poet from a pedant.

Couldn't tell a sasquatch from a seer.
Here are poncho'd lefties talking turkey.

Have a chaw of mesquite with your beer.
Couldn't tell a pimp from a pumpernickel.

Couldn't tell a bombardier from a bee.
Townes Van Zant is divided into three.

—

Another third's crossed the water,
trading his chaff-haired daughter for a fee.

Love becomes expedient
replaced by glugs of Tokay and a minor key.

Plight your troth, but plight it slant,
divorcee Townes Van Zant.

So batten down your capos, boys.
Chant a cry for the humble breed.

Build a chant from scree.
Townes Van Zant is divided into three.

Three Is Just A Better Form Of Two

Had Wild Bill Hickock
not turned his back to an open doorway
he'd never have sported that rose behind his ear

                        courtesy of Jack McCall esq,
               displayed that fan-tail of aces and eights
          or felt his face rebuff the sulphurous breath

of his opium vision - the snorting white buffalo of death
to be precise. They say the dispute
was over some unknown woman.

                  Binary oppositions always betray us.
               The good thief, the bad thief, vying,
for position as they are dying. The middle-man way beyond belief.

No-one plunges, no-one can go flying
without the pivot underneath
the see-saw - the rumour that goes off at a tangent

                      way beyond its own locale
                      like light from a far star
                  contingent to doubtful kings.

Just as on The Road To Abeline or Emmaeus
they sensed the significant other,
behind every lover

                  we always glimpse another
           attached to their ankle like a shadow.
             A triangle is only half a star

and no glance is as plangent,
nor any bolder, than the glance you steal
from over her boyfriend's shoulder.

Towards A Philosophy Of Speed

Baby, if the burden of being the fastest thing ever seen or heard
    is granted to the paper-plane or humming-bird
        hurtled down the central aisle of Concorde,

then a fat man running away
    from himself is the very definition of velocity,
        baby, even his aftermath-blur achieves solidity.

Nothing can ever be what it never was again.

Then this CCTV-footage shows us, not baby/ boy/man,
    baby, but loops of white-chalk failing to confine
        what flees its own outline like a fast cartoon

to still the cog-wheels of our intent
    so that we live, baby, always inside the moment
        before something happens and the moment after it hasn't.

That our eyes perceive colours at different speeds.
    If a conductor's baton was red instead
        of white, baby, the symphony they were
            conducting would proceed at a slightly slower speed,

- Baby. Nothing can ever be what it never was again -

so we might fuck, die, sleep, wake again
    in the time it takes the slowcoach moon
        to burn an inverse sun-spot through the curtain.

The Fabulists

Frank is no more to blame
    for his lame followers
than the wind through the firs,
    the furs of elderly dowagers out on the avenue
who are not to be blamed at all,
    taking their elegant pooches out for a stroll,
with hats as wrinkled as walnuts
    and hideous broaches

on rainy Thursday nights
    like senile Cinderellas crimped and counterfoiled.
No, Frank is not to blame
    for such lame fare. And no-one has the wherewithall
to say no to the bottle
    or the lure of a pearl-handled Derringer.
To a dowager hiding a Derringer in her stole.
    Eyes as tough as topaz. Eyes as brutal as quartz.

[He pronounces 'topaz' as 'towpath'.] Two fingers of the hard stuff.
    A doctor prods to tell him where it hurts.
There. And there. And there. There, there.
    Ouch. Even when being serious everything seems ersatz.
Frank certainly has his admirers,
    desperate to show how ordinary they are.
And God, they are.
    Ode to a Grecian Urn./Ode to a *Vic*-jar. Etc. Etc.

The bodegas and the lights. 5th Avenue.
    The waiter at his elbow waits
for a yellow cab. A man with a sign saying *Hertz*.
    Any old dowager, one of The Three Fates
along with their stained stoles and their virtue.
    So, the admirers of Frank -

> *Inversion. We must stamp out inversion*
> *from our prosody. We don't live in Arcady*
> *and this is real life, not some rhapsody*
> *translated from The Persian.*

So, Frank's admirers meet over instant coffee.
    But surely cafe society cannot exist

without the cafe? No, Frank's is as much to blame
    for his lame followers - these museum pieces-
as the wind through the firs,
    the liver-spots on the hands and faces
of elderly dowagers
    swathed as they are in mink-muffs and gold lame
out on the rainy avenue with their nieces. They persist.
    No, Frank is not to blame for such lame fare.

We may concur that the fabulists are elsewhere.

Of Books And Their Vicissitudes

1] El Desdichado Replay

Gerard de Nerval tugs gently on the silken leash that strays a
                mere metre
or so across The Luxembourg Garden gravel
pausing to contemplate his navel, the start of a novel
or the lop-sided length of his pet-lobster's claws.

He plucks a star-strewn lute for his errant lover.
He knows the glints in the brightest jewel
turn out to be its flaws.
That the stricken tower will

loosen the tongue of its bell. That the page and the night are
as black and white as jackdaws
and salt-petre. That time will tell. But the lobster

itself knows all too well that a revolution
can be fought and won in the time it takes him to travel
from one side of paradise to the other.

2] The Unauthorised Biography

You are deep in biography -the book arrived before
the corpse had cooled-lying on the deepest, threadbare sofa. So far
deep that you might not make the surface.
Suffice to say that you are deep. Deep in your lair.

So, to precis the story: the birth, the waif
grown to a rake then led astray; eros/agape; the beau in the
            feather-boa; the altar, the altercation;
the assignation with the slattern,
the split from the wife;

the Thanatossian glossary of pep-pills; the longeurs, jongleurs, the
            steep decline
-we can discern the usual pattern:
eros/agape; the gap, the life compiling sheaf by sheaf

until either you or he turn over
a new leaf -somewhere between the flyleaf or the endpapers
            -and suffer
the lack of each other. Put down the biography. Sleep.

3] The Weight

Apparently, the deep bow in my bookshelf is the weight
of my *Brewer's Dictionary Of Phrase & Fable* and my *Fontana
            Dictionary Of Modern Thought*
combined, so says my carpenter
standing amidst the heaps of Andrew Motion, the heaps of
            Harold Pinter.

Hard to say who's more agog,
-him or me- witness to this machine-gun spray of raw-plugs.
'See here' he says, 'in black and white we can see -Judas Tree
{Bot.} a leguminous tree of the genus Cercis

with pretty rose-coloured flowers along its branches, like
            blood-spots. Judas
is said to have hanged himself from a tree of this very genus
-C. Siliquastrum- hung himself by the neck until irrefutably dead.

31

Incidentally' he continues 'C. Occidentalis and C. Canadensis are the American version of the species- also known as 'the redbud'.

The Novel

    'Pleasure? Never touch the stuff'
said Malthraux darkly from under the brim of his panama.
    'Merely existing at the requisite level is enough,
breathing in then breathing out like the frangipani'
    The sea-breeze made the table-napkins salt-stiff.
'Also' he continued 'Pain animates
    where pleasure only sates'

    I sneezed at that as a flower blows its spores
to be carried by the wind to pollute another
    flower. He had caught me gazing down at my sugared croissant
with un-disguised aversion.
    With a flick of his wrist
and finger-click he ordered five side salads and an entree.
    'It's currently the fashionable itch' he re-began

    to dazzle with mediocrity
when actually its harder just to dazzle'.
    A gaggle of pale girls
in too-tight cerise costumes slapped through the sea-drizzle
    gingerly. 'Dig in, dig in'
he urged 'You're so thin you're almost an evasion of something'.
    One cerise costume darker near the lower notch.

    The striped awning and the guy-ropes. The boaters.
We might all be warm-up brush-strokes
    for *The Beach At Trouville*. 'Truth is vile'
said Malthraux' and massively overrated
    Honesty is a critical invention'.
I wondered if he ever said a sentence
    that wasn't a maxim. His whole life a whim.

        I stared down at the thief
of my eighth olive. The sky turned down the contrast.
        A cloud burst. The girls scatted like buckshot in a gust
as the drenches came. 'We have our parasol, our canopy
        as protection. There's no rain strong enough
to dilute a proper conversation'.
        Malthraux was hoarse. 'Though it might dilute the wine'.

        He still looked as prim
as a Penguin Classic. Yet there was indeed something faux
        about his elegant foulard and lion-headed walking-stick.
And why was his left arm in a sling?
        Always the expansive Epicurean
he lent forward to whisper in my ear. 'As you no doubt know
        The proper translation of *nouvelle* is *mostly nothing.*'

        The sun expanded. The rain withdrew.
But as rain-droplets made a mobile of our parasol,
        I knew that I was already through with Malthraux.
That I'd delete him in a single stroke
        even though he's served me well. He rose uncertainly
from the table. First burped, then farted. 'The root of *desire*
        is *being without a star*' I had him say over his shoulder. With
        that the bard departed.

The Plot

Discernably, is six foot long by three feet wide
of gently-tended, freshly-washed white gravel
and that's that. Except for this: that there are only two kinds of man,
                     the one who read
-s the first paragraph of a novel

first and the one who reads the last
paragraph first - a terrible sin for which he must atone.

And no-one yet is forewarned of the twist
in which a one-eyed man walks past the plot, carrying a salmon

The Smell Of Books

Apparently, opening up a cod-fish
the pseudonymous Charles Yellowplush
found in its maw a duodecime work
by one John Firth-
a treatise on the worth of penitence.

The pong of dissolute authors
can overpower
the nostrils. Avoid risk.
Always wear a smog-mask.
A better policy may be complete avoidance.

Though the febrile reek of dog daisies
can outstink even us,
its *50 Key Contemporary Thinkers* idling by a vase
that overpowers.
Don't inhale. Keep your distance.

For some, the relative snuff
of haiku is enough.
Watch out. This can provoke levity,
a minimal Zen-like brevity
or trance.

By comparison, philosophy is smack
or popping all the E's of George Perec.
The amyl-nitrate
Cities Of The Red Night
covertly pleading for temperance.

But my own mien
is inhaling *The Song Of Solomon,*
like pollen-filled air
or a woman's hair
drenched in myhrr or frankincense.

You follow the wafted spores
through rotating doors
and out into the city - all its smells
singing in your nostrils:
the stink of love, the smell of books, the recompense.

Ammonius Saccas

Simultaneously, he is inhaling olbas-oil
in boiling vapours from a flayed *Nescafe* jar

reading about Plotonius or Origen in Alexandria
in the exceptionally thorough

The Passion Of The Western Mind by Richard Tar
-nas. He's in its thrall.

He's sleepy and prone to pressure in the sinuses -little inverted commas
inside the eye-cavity, vein-blue

and also prone
to the night-buses running, the No 3 or No 2

and urban foxes emerging out of man-holes
-their shrill baby-cries shaking the dew.

Ammonius Saccas, so Tarnas tells us,
about whom little is known

taught students of both Christian and Pagan persuasion,
helped forge Rome to save such sinners as us.

Peacock-screams from the city farm;
the curlew of a car-alarm.

Later, he comes upon a particular
passage from a lesser-known novel by Paul Theroux

as the No 3 or the No 2 Nightbus painfully ascend the hill.
The stained coverlet, the stained towel,

the improvised samovar of olbas-oil,
by all that is holy or profane

he sleeps conscious of un-blocked sinuses
and Ammonius Saccas.

Is This Isthmus A Land-Mass
Or Is This Land-Mass An Isthmus?

Unaccustomed as we are, bear
with us as we try, unerringly, to construct a convincing paradiso
        terrestre,
a paradiso for these times. Firstly we need the fog, the foen, the fret,
the orioles, the pines, but not that
water-tower, that rusting eyesore,
those eggplants and those limes, both lit as if some still-life Rousseau
everything so easy on the eye
as everything is easy in these climes.
No. Drop the fog. It would only wrinkle your notebook
in which is writ, if you look,
Ex Libris Captain Nemo in blue biro.
Add the singing hinges of a corncrake some water-fowl or
mainly, mostly stones -shale,
pumice, obsidian so they cascade in steppes and shelves
down to the ocean shore. Our soundtrack is a mix of kettle
-drums and oboes. Foxes in an aviary. Our theme-tune? Something
        nouvelle
-vague or urban-pastoral, say, *New York Tendaberry*
by Laura Nyro. We've already built the obligatory jetty
with its rickety stilts and slats stepping gingerly into the water.
Ought we
to raise an A-frame and a weak sun?
A gazebo? A glazed pavilion? No. Drop the jetty. Too Malcolm Lowry. Too
        Dollorton.
We need no carefully secreted Mescal-bottles
lying behind the columbine on this isthmus. No down-at-heel Consul
with throw-up on his shoes stalking past the rude stockade
where a yearling colt karate-kicks its paddock.
Maybe we feel as isolated
as aphids on a lily-pad.

Yet still we watch him risk a safety-match to stir
the dying embers of the fire.
See his glow-worm hand all orange from the inside,
hear the embers say:

> *The Five Great Trancendentalists*
> *couldn't clear a privet hedge*
> *any better than a hen.*
> *So make you mark neither*
> *on the mainstream nor the edge.*

Useless then to dream to be asway
in the swinging hammock of the wide bay
the lacklustre estuary. Yet easier still to live for or upon
the slow-release tart-tang of blackberries and mere sunshine,
the blank, implacable water, the distinct lack of canaries.
Un-accustomed, precisely, as we are.

Ode : *Rapid Eye Movement*

*And Ralph Eugene Meatyard lived
in Normal, Illinois*

Not Jo'berg, Illinois
as recounted by Tom Waits-
posing as a woman
wth his wife, with his wife
man and boy

*No, Ralph Eugene Meatyard lived
in Normal, Illinois*

He'd pour over silly Champagne,
notebooks of terrible names
and masked tots,
backwoods Spinoza The Lens-Grinder
opposed to the hoi-polloi.

*Yes, Ralph Eugene Meatyard lived
in Normal, Illinois*

Not Champagne, Illinois,
that bootleg by Mr Zee
-Zimmerman or Zukofsky-
using breath, using light, using light, using breath
to descry

*No, Ralph Eugene Meatyard lived
in Normal, Illinois*

His ear would attend on The Andrew's Sisters
singing Poe's *The Raven*
[*Ulalume* on the flip]
but he never read, no never read
The Oddyssey

Yes, Ralph Eugene Meatyard lived
in Normal, Illinois

Not Athens, Georgia nor Athens, Greece
but bricks suspended in air
on the cover of *Flowers & Leaves*
-poems by,
Davenport, Guy. £1.20.

No, Ralph Eugene Meatyard lived
in Normal, Illinois

Too late, too ill to annoy
Lucybelle Crater And Her Good Friend Lucybelle Crater In
             The Grape Arbor
thinning inside his wife's smock
in a flash, in a flash
of joy

Yes, Ralph Eugene Meatyard lived
in Normal, Illinois

Wallace Stevens At The Oboe

[1]

Dusk and your absence
swells to a palpable stanchion.

By *Selectadisc* the bus
swerves in an unpeopled station

as a frisbee absentmindedly
flys through the pebbled washroom

where dusky absinthe
is swilled by culpable henchmen

and frisky aperetifs
are squandered by a capable freshmen

whose key phrases add blunt
swipes at a statistician

as doors open on alabaster and porcelain,
a graffited S.W.A.L.K and a pulp novel heroine.

[2]

Days seem abstract
enough to make their own form of hum-drum.

A disc emits bad synth
-sounds like a soiled CD Rom.

A dazed woman frisked by a warden
sweating in an unpalatial room

-where the dust of absolute aeons
flees the air-freshener-

kisses a dizzy, absconded
squaddy, goes A.W.O.L like Captain Flashman

and, dissed, feels absurd
swearing at an old pal in pidgeon French

while a roue with angina and a plumpy ingenue
congess with dumb-assed aplomb.

[3]

We should not inveigle but oust the rich, blame
their girth, their swanky per capita

allowances, their modal license to flash,
to flash their dolorous monies.

The Great Arab
mooted a loan to a hermetic franchise

but was damaged and obstructed,
deferred, bought, battered by the Dow Jones

Index. Whiled away time for a woeful tax-disc,
up to his shins in lamentable begonias,

their deafening ripples. Now an organ of The State
which dared to war on want

is dismissed by a dour ambassador
who swills pale people from the envoy room.

[4]

Pancho wore a sharp-angled poncho
and would pooh-pooh each *bon mot*

and its pitiable intention. Even the stench of the sun.
He'd say: 'All's flush, unchaste,

each wears an incomparable mask. Peep-oh.'
Yet one wind-rush of her musk

would render him a blind man
in every orifice blinder than a senile Sancho

Panza. Hi-ho. Complete surrender. He's buy her
amethysts, conch-shells, Wim Wenders

videos, couches from The Bay Of Biscay but
she hid, in secrecy.

The wrench left its mark. Thus the contrary wench
was easily head honcho.

[5]

Is it delinquent to note what my Mentor
meant or was it misheard

his absurd address? When I knew more
I knew less and how to abhor

my Mentor for occupying before. All's risk.
No lone peacock feather is a bird.

It's a rote torment. To sleep in the lee
of a spreading tree and sip its sap,

it shadows all. It blots the sky.
Should we not seek redress? We're not Orient

to the Mentor when we sup
his bitter curd. Yet birds twitter

in his lee most brilliantly. And the Mentor
knows even he is over-awed by the terrible sea.

[6]

We must never divert from the ostracised phlegm
that hurts, perennially, as words hurt

worse than flesh. It's the longing to belittle
all flesh as dimwitted man

when he is a grand parable
for whom the enfranchised many

flair in a democracy of fire and air,
obscene, unheard, swatted. A herd, an aristocracy.

This is the benchmark. Flesh is a penchant
for which we risk, fail and flash

briefly. But the lumpy congress lacks ingenuity
like numb asses while the chastised few

look to some far star
as a trenchant asterisk.

[7]
So he divests the ostrich-plumes
that girt her swart perineum

allowing the little odalisque of flesh
to flash like a diminutive moon

with an arable grunt
and the moan of a muted French horn.

She's damasked as an obsidian
bird, a sward, an inverted, plush-buttoned chaise-longue.

When The Dame asks the woebegone
bard to shun the unpalatable sun

he deliciously replies: 'Dear One, orphan of an absentee,
sweet as a wanton plum,

it is dusk and your absence
swells to a palpable stanchion'.

Birds And Their Shadows
after Ezra Pound

The souls of birds
are their shadows skating across the lawns
like skimmed slates.

Without the ballast of their
shadows they couldn't fly.

She steps out of the undone duvet
from the far room in knickers and bra to tell me:
'Guess where I went to
in dream - Ohio, though
I've never been to Ohio
where the roads are as long as you imagined and...'

There was an ox-bow
lake and sixteen picnic blankets spread
but empty?

'Yes, how did you...'

And you skinny-dipped in the reservoir
while the petrol-pump attendants
wolf-whistled from the sandbank,
their yellow rain-macs shiny as seals and...

'I felt how many salt tear
-s below me, buoyed me up...'

She must be speaking
of the novels of Don DeLillo, I thought
or some other great American.
Light as the green souls of birds
flashing across the grass.

The Measurement Of Quims
after Rufinus

Diana The Hunter's
was neat as a skiff
bobbing on the little

loch of her lap. Whereas
Phoebe's was more a trireme,
leaving its wheat-blonde V

of a wake
and splendidly be-quiffed.
Sylphides', though

was the scary craft to row,
black-lacquered gondola across The Styx
with sleek

fur like a jaguar. Mere mortal
-s might drown
or never return.

I can't swim
so have to trust these craft-
their many variations on the theme.

But yours
is where I quaff
the deepest draught-

coracle, catamaran, liferaft.

The Family

There, there. Whether
born out of love, luck or ingenious error
can you hear
one ghost or eminence-gris concur
with the other
as, blinded inside the white and boiling square
they slightly flicker and stir?
Just as soon as you discern a certain feature
it will absent itself and blur
each indefinite tibia or fibia
bone-grafted onto the ether.
If you happen to be looking for a father
then maybe you should look further
as this one seems too thin to hover
over a son. And this mother
cannot help but smother
her daughter
who, apropos of nothing, is sly as a cantilever,
defining the air between them more
than anything they might share
-which could be a lock, a straw, a strand of hair
slipped inside a pillow cover,
a tarnished candelabra,
some silverware,
all heirlooms without an heir.
What, no patent frigidaire,
no bowl of catmint, lint, no copper colander?
No cellular-phone, no Masked Conquistador,
no cellophane shrink-wrapped slightly bruise-blue pear?
No Expelair?
No. It is her duty to mither
the unruly brood with a lacklustre

kind of care. His duty to leer
straight ahead at the witless viewer
or wheel out the scare
-story of The Bogeyman or monster
who, dwelling beneath the stair
has a dire need to devour
such wild, unsleepy sires.
See here, inside his bone-filled lair,
this paw-print, this hank of fur,
the reek of sulphur and tar.
Or take some time to mutter
a fervent prayer for
Mrs Cecilia Bugg, wife of Henry Bugg Esq
who is buried here
or so this monument says in seriphed alabaster.
They might whisper 'My dystopia is better
than your distopia' or
'Who's style's as austere as Paul Auster?'.
We should here, in turn, observe the observers,
born to mutter
nothings, to sift and grimly inter -
the bolshy contents of a *Wonderbra,*
the plotlines of ER,
the struck-through dates on last year's *Pirelli* calender
drifting through a hinter
-land that is eternally winter.
Look here-
the son is spraying himself with *Christian Dior*
in front of the triple mirror
of his mother's dresser
gently wielding her onyx-backed hair
brush bear
-ing her fine-blond hairs,
tripled, womanly, not yet a teenager,

maybe swathed in otter-fur
and sheer tights with a deft, downwards ladder
up which me might well climb to the land of Ur.
His face is pale as refined flour,
as cool as Catherine Deneuve in *Belle de Jour*.
He'll pose by the antimacassar,
round-shouldered, thuggish as a tapir.
By the cowed wysteria
which grows more aslant each year.

Who bears the pallbearers? Who hauls the pallbearer's where?

Yes, the family is here
to greet us -stand and stare-
each one misplaced somewhere
between a foetus and a cadaver.
Each a ghost or eminence-gris who can barely concur
with the other
that what they share is a fissure,
a tremendous, terrible flaw
-whether born out of luck or ingenious error-
to briefly flicker and flare
inside each boiling square
where a secret door
opens onto another secret door
and the frisson you get is never
the frisson you ask for. So there.

Of Love And Its Vicissitudes

1] Pliny The Elder

Sulkily, he strikes a match against the arching alder,
singing a white-hot outline along the underside of the longest branch
like a current, the solitary elder
-berry nearby a sudden network. Someone has hit the 'on' switch.

Instantly he sees Rita Hayworth in *Gilda,*
that hair like a lit-up torch,
her very décolléte seeming to spill her
into his lap, prone as he is on the agitated couch, which

in turn, fetches up another redhead -one Hilda or Tilda,
he forgets quite which- whose beehive seemed to scorch
the very sky. He'd told her, beneath a not-so-dissimilar alder

that what with her long, white body and spry red hair she was every
inch
an unstruck match, that he 'held a torch' for her, that Pliny The
Younger was actually older than Pliny The Elder
and much else besides. They never kept in touch.

2] The Peachstone

Deftly, in the hallway, we catch up with him mid-thought, thinking
about the skill
of half-inching a paw-paw or persimmon
then re-arranging the fruit inside her fruitbowl
so none seemed gone, when, buried between grapefruit and plum,
he comes upon the lodestone.

So he throws it away from him, far-flung,
as far away as possible, beyond his own reach and ability
thinking it won't take root. He's wrong.
A stone's throw away grows up a sturdy peach tree.

Now its peaches hang,
fur-soft, heavy, tantalisingly
close - their moist circumferences, the sly divide of each.

He wants to bite into each one,
the juice running own his chin, his ribs, his leg
until his teeth hit on the dark-red stone. Please, don't make him beg.

3] Serial Pillows

Each time I woke and rose
from serial pillows
to find the very same bullet weighted on my tongue,
the nickel-plated tang

redolent of powder
and velocity. Each time I'd remember the ricochet off my body-armour
up into the air, my upwards stare, it landing lamely-smoking inside
      my open
mouth. There was shock but very little pain.

Each time a new flame or an old flame
flickers and flares up from the compromised divan
and breezes out trailing a burgundy-red, diaphanous nightgown

in order to powder her face or tie up her hair
it gives me time to recover, to recover the bullet from
its hiding place, to see if my name is engraved there.

Sleepwalking For Beginners

Apparently -my light, my love- they part the drip-dry bayberry
to survey the scene : the panting alsation occupying
the pyramid-shaped shadow
growing from the corner of the house

that makes the big lawn mauve or even mauver.
They say we walk, nay, glide -my love, my light-
across the gravelled pathway through the elderberry or wolfberry
or whatever - hackberry possibly-

where two griffins
sit white-knuckled on their plinths.
That a dozen or so lawn-sprinklers throw their liquid
Mobius-loops
heavily and reluctantly

as we essay out across their vast desmene.
Apparently, worried they can't contain us,
-our love, our light-
their hirelings fix pedometers onto our heels

in order for them to ascertain
the unaccounted kilometres of sleep,
such is the breadth and swerve
of our meanderings. Though we always come back,
apparently,

at inexplicable hours, -
certain night-moths feeding at
the ink-well of your clavicle, the gulp of my Adam's apple-
for examination. Sometimes you say 'cicatrix'

and sometimes I say 'lubricous'
and other words from a sly and elusive lexicon
    too difficult to tag. Apparently, all we remember
        -some light, some love- is coming awake to this:

    the sting-stink of ammonia, the marrow-deep fault-line of our jaws,
that and the mutt returning,
    its wet-nosed sniff of the real, *Astroturf* compressing crisply
        under its paws.

Flight

Enter Mrs Esmerelda Tanager
semi-illegal alien- out of Africa, Tanganika, elsewhere-
her wrap-design a fine bird of paradise,
observed, as if in hides, by green-tinged beams, with x-rays, two-way
    mirrors.

Passengers meet and part like globules of mercury.
Tinny announcements bee-buzz in the Tannoy:
A butterfly caught is a butterfly lost, thresholds vanish as thresholds are
    crossed, neither are for you, neither, you who are
    made from cuttle-ink and ether.
Mdme Tanager is crossing hers, sweaty, buoy

-ant, blood jolting to a *Sony-Walkman*'ed Fela Kuti remix
when the *Fetherlite* in her colon
containing -one gram? one ounce?- splits into a seamless seam

as she bursts through Arrivals
un-announced, to face a man with a cardboard sign scrawled ALBION,
the shot bird taking off in fourteen directions at once.

Low Maintenance Roof Garden

We take the air of our low-maintenance roof garden
this austere quad our best line of defence
from the smoky street where we hear arteries harden.

Honesty seems a new form of pretence
for here is hardly either Avalon or Eden.
Yet this gravel reach can seem a wild expanse.

We splay on deckchairs wilting in the sun,
as window-boxes bear the flowering quince,
the flowering plum. We live above neon, shop-signs, gargoyles,
                    gorgons.

If you leap for joy do not leap over the fence
of our low-maintenance roof-garden
and one did once and some have done so since.

The street below. The sky above. The garden in between
with only barren stones as any sustenance,
-mica-chips, wave-smoothed glass, obsidian-

we lie on these hard stones doing penance
for not having a warm shoulder to cry on.
A shingle beach half way up the sky has the appearance

of the temporary. Yet we mark our territory aeon after aeon
and reaquaint ourselves with innocence,
lying between the stars and municipal bins.

If there's anything to take we take it on sufferance.
Taking the air of our roof-garden.
It's night. We hear a noise. Pardon? What? The noise is silence

or dawn bringing the black hat of the traffic warden
to pin the law on the windscreen's crazy flourescence
below. We sit tight in our low-maintenance roof-garden.

Arctic Fleece

Two old crones, two crows
      overhead gabbing in the runneled air out of Seven Sisters
one to the other: 'I'm on the prowl
      for an Arctic Fleece for Jacob
or Janice' - no flim-flam, no caprice -
      just the way desire solidifies into stub-end scented pavements,
the ability to wield an Air-Freshener

like a cosh or a can of Mace-
      two grande dames on a quest for an artic fleece.
Not hooded in ermine or Royal
      mink[they've been fleeced] alpaca but fake-fur
to warm his/her hidden Sony-Walkman
      to their temporal
lobes -that is Janice's, Jacob's- to keep the doctor away -the
      runnelled air

out of Seven Sisters, the way warm collects
      between a woman
and a duck-down duvet. Thus do Jacob/Janice desire
      an arctic fleece and thus do certain desiccated duchesses
strike out for Seven Sisters in the runnelled air
      as if Seven Sisters were actually
The Arab Quarter or Sainte-Sulpice -

the nonchalant boulevards of Paris, their
      Gitane-scented pavements-
yet the palpable notion of grace
      might still suffice, even here. A fire-hydrant,
a man-hole cover, wrecked hollyhocks. A man, intent on loitering
      maybe Jacob on the cusp between
with-holding and release

-deep 'into himself,
    man' -the blood-cell red of his lining
Sony-Walkman'd ears, pupils expanding and protracting
    by *Super-Drug* or the 7/11, even. Whereas Janice is pure desire,
pure runnelled air out of Seven Sisters, her silver-fringe
    and fake-fur taking
the tinge off the evening, project

-ing it onto two bats, too bags,
    haggling an artic fleece. 'The lowest price is the right price'
A sign says DO NOT DISTURB,
    a three-legged dog is running
its three-legged race
    to the side of the curb-tick-tick-tick- a curbstone smelling
        of *Senior Service-*
will not deflect them, endlessly bolstered by

the fay upholstery
    of your actual, genuine artic fleece -Jacob and Janice,
some nephew or niece ['who'll deplore us
    if we fail'] doomed to repeat themselves and cruise for
        Strawberry E's
supplied to them by Dr Ronald Ayre out of Seven Sisters
    where, overhearing the very words 'artic fleece'
might conjure up some ice-palace

-ice-flames caught in a fireplace of ice,
    ice-particles, magma and pumice -suddenly released up an
        air-vent
by way of a smelting. So that these Old Dears
    begin to sprint-
sprint through the runnelled air out of Seven Sisters
    past Cell-phone ads and arrears
into the covered arcades for an arctic fleece.

Two Silver Birches

Hard to get a purchase
on these two silver birches
high above the over-run
garden. One, the taller

attended by a magpie,
the other, smaller, by a sparrow.
Particularly
how one leans its body

just ever so slightly
away from the other.
To hold such a position continually
would bring an ache

in the arms to end all aches.
But one need not be
a tree-sprite
or dryad

to know how tired
the night get
-s or limbs so heavy
that a dew-drop breaks

a bough. And though
against this calming sky
both seems content enough
in a certain

light
they appear to be as temporary
as blown bonfire-smoke
or a rash of hail.

Nevertheless
what grace
to hold their
ground above the over-run garden

chaffing gently against each other
like those in the know.
The one, attended by a nightingale.
The other by a crow.

The Scene Of My Former Triumph

[1]

Had been mooted as a venue. The sun looked
like something from Andrew Marvell
as it palpitated my eye-flowers, their periphery, where
two pseudo-Japanese warriors shrugged off their pixels

in intergalactic wars
and brown sauce was proffered but declined.
Much here is a subterfuge for what never happened anyway
and all of us need the required amount

of mundanity for time in the malls. And though I finally
got a handle on Augusta at the winter palace
-her oboe-shaped backside plangent against the snow-

mostly I was just mooching around
at the scene of my former triumph,
whatever triumph that was.

[2]

The gargoyle on the parapet
was designed by a triumphalist
to make us feel weighty and subject to beasts and demons,
that feeling that all our scars have yet

to be stitched in, shady beneath the burgeoning subterfuge.
The required amount of mundanity
got a handle on Augusta
like something out of inter-galactic wars. And though I finally

mooted a venue, plangent against the snow,
the sun looked like brown sauce
proffered and then declined

as it palpitated two pseudo-Javanese warriors
at the scene of their periphery
whatever triumph that was.

[3]

O the leak of little phrases
attempting to resist their own beginning
like a river running away from mountain and cloud
to frolic inside the disallowed

like a playground truant, errant, spent,
as if, as if, designed by a triumphalist
for whom the modernity of the parapet was subject
to beasts and demons that made him feel weighty

as their oboe-shaped backsides. Does it ever stop and pause-
the river, I mean - not even
for Heraclitus and his brilliant leaf?

He is loafing around and stitching in his scars
from a former triumph
whatever triumph that was.

[4]

Christ was mooted as a brilliant leaf,
luxurious but shakeable eventually,
his sense of baffled epiphany and noble cause
made him feel weighty and attempt

to resist their own beginnings as if, as if
designed by a triumphalist
for loafing and stitching his scars. His subjects
were beasts and demons who never stopped to pause

at the river running away from mountain or cloud
or the weeping willows
shrugging off their pixels, proffering

and declining. We least expect
this subterfuge which never happened anyway
like the scene of my former triumph, whatever triumph that was.

Remembering The Ilex Tree

that was never yours, not even briefly,
    and most probably never will be
is the kind of hurt or glow
    [where does a hurt become a glow- at which point
or vice-versa?] that any well-versed man
    might nurse

like a memory of the 2A night-bus
    [whose kingdom stretched beyond thought]
where tree-tops combed the window
    and his own face reflected
fluid and mercury-swirled in the burnished seat-rail
    as the Dandelion & Burdock bottle

worried the full length of the upper deck,
    rolling and returning
as the trees make their litany:

>*the cool lurch*
>*and sway of a silver birch,*
>*the mighty oak,*
>*stolid hiding place*
>*of geeks and princes, each knot a haunted face.*
>*The crab-apple,*
>*monkey-puzzle,*
>*the stripling sycamores meshed on the estate*
>*whose*
>*towerblocks are named after trees*
>*-Willow, Ash and Alder-*
>*those desolate*
>*arbors*
>*whose trees are harbours in the sea*

> *of the sky... all those*
> *Greco-Roman fables*
> *that feature the dryad, tree-woman, tree-sprite,*
> *spirit of Avalon and Arcady,*
> *-brought bang up to date, or not quite*
> *by David Lynch's Twin Peaks in the character*
> *of the log-lady-*
> *Demeter*
> *and the rituals of Spring, all addled, all*
> *gone to blight...*

But the ilex tree is different, it begins elsewhere
    in a time beyond this time
when the night-bus didn't run and the kingdom knew no bounds

that a well-versed man
    could not patrol to the brink of his own desmene.
Not for neon or petrol, camouflage, buckshot but
    the sweet scent of the ilex tree
that isn't yours and never will be
    not even briefly.

Horse Longtitudes

Surprisingly, when I happ'd upon the foal,
this gangly, piebald quadruped was tentatively splaying its legs
contraywise to all four corners of the earth. By thought-transference
        I could almost feel
them straining and groaning like tent-pegs,

their painful metamorphosis -there a collapsed tripod,
thence a four-tined fork
that might pitch air or light but never hay, always rising and
        collapsing, self-tripped
in the fern-filtered clearing where I lay, nosing the pliant bark

of a tall, concealing tree-bole-maybe a jay-filled pine-
its pine-cones seeming like microphones
rebuffing the sly feedback of needle and breeze, until, stunned

I noticed its aniseed-pupil, also its sulphurous nostril
jet-black, coal-black, almost bolted through it, and felt less prone to
        wonder why the wind made four mini-diversions
around the hooves of this fly-bothered, sun-flayed foal.

Just Passing Through

[1]

everyone wears this
internal waistcoat, with chain
and ticking fob-watch

[2]

like some butterfly
in negative, wings parched dry
with spar-white markings

[3]

caterpillar-like
Steve McQueen flew the wild fence
as Prometheus

[4]

Nabakov or E
-lizabeth Bishop's *Man-Moth*
scorched to a pale fire

[5]

lizards into coach
-men, buds into chokecherries
Ovid in exile

[6]

and on and on and
on. Zeus would court the lovely
speckled Selene

[7]

not, for once, in the
form of a swan, but himself
a myth-maker hoist

[8]

on his own petard.
Strictures pin the thing alive
5 X 7 X 5

[9]

two white moons moon as,
on all fours, Selene ass
-umes the position

[10]

mons lunar and quiffed
a big blue see-thru striptease
little lush pupae

[11]

firework then zilch -day
spent drowning in *Liebfraumilsch*
chased by a puppy

[12]

the fiction of skin
betraying the bones below
might have us undone

[13]

in a shirt of fire
by courtesy of Nessus
or a cabbage-white

[14]

on a kimono.
Two geishas kiss a mirror
and are each other.

[15]

Rorschach-blot or what?
Man to flower, Echo in
-to stone, Narcissus

[16]

into himself. Be
-hold bleached Anorexia
the Goddess of ribs

[17]

doth entreat you to
swap your heart for a waistcoat
eaten by moths.

Welcome To _____, Twinned With_____

Two swallows nest behind a CCTV camera.
An immobile black stallion. The torn beach of a billboard.

'That crowd-noise might be fighting in the street. O to be as
                debonair
as wine-soaked Guy DeBord'.

That cowboy dressed in rayon. That tagger's lasso. That hush in
                the air
as if the away side has scored.

Three Avatars

1] Mado Raban Reprise

Irrefutably, she hit the highest notes ever heard,
hit the roof of the highest aria like the rarest bird inter-bred
        with a computer -
-a flotilla at full tilt-shattering tier after tier after tier
of supposedly shatter-proof champagne glasses stacked one
        inside the other to overshoot

even the highest note in The Queen Of The Nights' solo
from *The Magic Flute*,
a passage they're since transposed downwards
to allow lesser singers to still collect awards

for grazing in the lower registers. But the lymph-nodes
of her immaculate throat
played up, gave out

and they laid her out in a shallow trench
without much fuss or palaver. No-one built monuments,
composed palinodes
or thought to save her. Just something I thought I'd mention.

2] Salvador Dali : *The Sick Child [1914-18]*

If 'seeing is inventing' then Dali's The Sick Child
with arched, all-knowing eyebrows has re-invented me
for she has turned her back on the dappled, mauve-blue sea
as if the evening had suddenly chilled,

on the canary who once sniffed gas for a long-dead miner
and will now no longer sing, no longer
sing for me, me or anyone, on the unfinished plate of *esgargots*
the waiter has taken away

-small wonder that her pencil-sharpened fingers are four years older
than her face-
on the red yacht and the yellow yacht with smudges for prows
[what cargoes they could bring, what cargoes]

to stare out the wild blue yonder of 'why me?'
with a stare no wine-dark Dr Collin's tonic could cure,
the Y of her sub-sonic 'why?' -a wishbone, a water-diviner.

3] The Wellspring

Diligently, follow if you will, Mr Charles Olson -
delicate man-mountain, sniffing an asphodel,
worrying over immortal Sappho fragments
at Watchhouse Point

tall as doors yet teasing out the breath-lines,
part-hangman, part-Delphic Oracle,
not knowing if anyone gets, if they get at all
his continental-drift, his elemental kingfisher, which, diving
underwater

lets its long-held breath breathe life into the line,
so that the line holds up as long
as he holds oxygen, the next one inhaling the next one and so on

until The Master
merely curls inside the pupil
like an activating germ, like doubt, the worm, the wellspring.

Serendipity Ode

After taking a Strawberry E
at an illicit rave
the young man saw Brixton Hill as Parnassus.

The Privatised Water Companies
have
issued a ban on clouds and garden hoses.

A 1950's
beehive
is no longer a symbol for largesse.

An ilex tree
blooms from a pauper's grave
by process of photosynthesis.

Barbie
-sales shoot off the graph
following *Playboy* centrefold poses.

Gaston Bachelard's notion of 'reverie'
forgives
the poet his tendency to excess.

The amount of nudity
on the Algarve
has given rise to voyeurs becoming cancerous.

'True beauty'
said Robert Graves
'is worship of the moon Goddess Isis'.

BT
would have us believe
that silence is a form of neurosis.

The Dandy
imperiously-depraved,
asks the loss-adjustor to tally up his losses.

By cruel decree
the High Queen made a dozen servants weave
six neckties and six nooses.

On the shores of The Black Sea
the seventh wave
was a creamy veil of laces.

Unfortunately
this year Christmas Eve
will be cancelled due to tax increases.

Lorca met his Gethsemane
in an olive grove-
a fabulous sestina ripped to pieces.

Manchester City
were deprived
of a classic victory by a series of searching passes.

Doggedly
the Steelworker's Union drove
a hard bargain with 57 compromises.

Sent out over the endless sea
the tiny dove
returned with a sheaf of freehold leases.

Muhammad Ali
was a wicked blur of gloves-
part burning bush, part Moses.

Attendance at University
has vastly improved
since the advent of the 25 word thesis.

In this anthology: John Ashbery,
John Ash, Rita Dove
and keeping strange company, Herbert Lomas.

Virility
isn't measured by multiple loves,
but gurgling noises.

The naked body
found hanging in the architrave
was said to have perished from 'natural causes'.

Walt Disney
in his mania to live
is cryogenically frozen and never decomposes.

Either take LSD
or browse through Peter Redgrove's
The Moon Disposes.

One certainty:
we are all the slaves
of The Dark Angel With Wings Of Inverted Commas.

Propping up his TV-
is a Gideon Bible, Asian Babes, *Palgraves
Golden Treasury* and *Roget's Thesaurus.*

The Un-American Activities Committee-
proof positive
that the winner sometimes loses.

The Archbishop of Canterbury
never forgave
the nuns who chose to wear trousers.

Serendipity
does not behave
by way of laws or logical process.

Giacommetti
said the purpose of having a shave
was metamorphosis.

In the windy inner-city
everything is dying on the move
from crisis to crisis.

One condition of Post Modernity
is that love
becomes a pair of *Haagen Das* ices.

Reputedly
when Rimbaud had his leg removed
it sprouted roses.

Cul-de-Sac

Apparently, I proceeded in an easterly direction, with no lack
of temerity. Saw the wild bayberry-blossom
of the sink-estate.
A stranger uprooted and said: 'Not that way, mate, it's a cul-de-sac'.

He placed great stress on the 'de'. There was now no turning back.
By then, we were headlong into each other
you, humbled below me, turned the other way, your shoulder-blades
                      moving like skimmed slates over tawny water.

To sleep with anyone is risk,
-the virus of love, the virus of obligation- the fear of being opened to
                      any turn
of events. Strange then that after, you formally donned a sleep-mask
as if not wanting to witness a burglar break suddenly into your home.

There are those who believe that, as it and us share swirling molecules,
                  we can walk through solid matter.

D-d-d- don't wait for me by the spider-web scintillations
of the broken kiosk. I won't be back.

The Critics Who Failed To Define Their Own Epoch

still wrote Ex-Libris ____
    in blue biro on the flyleaves of seminal texts
in those days - those days of long-tailed crows in the trees-
    with the weight, the weight of the self, as ascribed by a trembly X,

as if they had seized on a micro-dot,
    but missed the onslaught of *The Fontana Dictionary
Of Modern Thought*
    bending and bowing each bookshelf, as it ought. My

comic-serious friend-let's call him Bloch, Bloch or maybe
    Block-had attempted to define the era
or epoch for himself as 'when heat made the dragonflies flirty
    enough to mate in mid-air

so that sloth and ambition
    were held in a perfect tension.' If I had
any time, in those days, then I had time for Block or Black and Vera,
    his very own'
concierge'- rumoured to be a demieverge with whom he shared

an abode. Back then, the young men sported copies of Deleuze and
    Guattari
    or Lyotard's *Libidinal Economy* peeking out of their pocket-tops,
    just enough so you knew,
knew that they knew, or actually
    didn't. The sky was always a tinge of aqua-blue

as if reflecting a swimming-pool and the critics who had failed to define
    their epoch lay on lilos
or rose imperiously to the top of their profession
    as chancellors or Chairs like long-tailed crows flapping into the
            trees

whilst Black or Bleak
    lay undiscovered, indolent, someone seminal for whom
hindsight had not yet streaked
    far enough away from

to look back upon with any proper appraisal. See he's there by the fish-
            stalls
    and the florists, the Municipal-bins, the council-clock
falling parallel
    with the moon -turning up his *Pac-a-Mac*

against a gust of rain. He will leave the cinema, blinking into the
            cinema of evening. Meanwhile
    the critics feed or confide in the cognocenti on a need-to-know
basis. They don't deconstruct Oasis or Donatello. They dribble
    in their text-books. Ex-libris. Blue biro.

Whilst hyper-critics of the hyper-real map the scope
    of the available terrain
[vis a vis Baudrillard's notion of television making everything seem like
            an archaic envelope]
    enough to sum it all up- I envisage Bloke or Bleck drain

ing a styrex cup, letting the bubbles gently addle his nose.
    Free verse or prose? Is it iambic? Trochaic? Him peering
                  imperiously at the manuscript in crypt or cafe.
A Plato's
    cave. His A-Z is fraying at the edges. There's fresh signs of ruin
        in his face.

And the critics? The critics who failed
    to define their own epoch now lay
on lilos or deep in quicklime-trenches. Years pass. Whole years until
    'these days' actually get to mean 'those days'.

I've lost touch with Mr Bloch but happen to bump into Vera or was it
        Verity?
    -they'd since split *-split apart like a buck-shot quince-* was how
        she put it, but yes,
she knew his digs off an alleyway where the graffiti left no room for
        graffiti
    and they made fires

from dedicated benches. Funnily enough, as some kind of spontaneous
        memento
    for 'those days' the young men and women still sport Deleuze and
        Guattari
gathering in the cafe's like long-tailed crows.
    This very night, Bloch or Bloke and I will meet for a soiree,

- espressos igniting the tables
    with black light. The waitress -Basque-Separatist, un-kissed,
        will note
Block's throwaway comments in a marble
    -patterned note

-book and later launch a play. [Reasonable first notices. A brief season
　　　on Broadway]. We'll leave, tipsy, leaving her a tip, a tribute,
and stroll through the periphery of this city -all manholes and arson-
　　　talking shop. Loot

-ing the entire shop, morelike. We'll take in the rust-coloured roofs, that
　　　　　　　　　　　　　　　long,
　　　sanguine hound-dog panting under a bay tree.
Municipal bins. See escalators, rising,
　　　　　take them. Block will say 'And if this seems too much 'closure' for
　　　　　　　　　　such a complicated story

held in a pre-tensile tension
　　　by a kind of sloth or ambition that the critics of this era or epoch
　　　　　　　　would always
fail to define then so be it. The moon is still the moon.
　　　It's closing time. And if I'm unapologetic, then I'm sorry'

Tall Iced De-Caffeinated Latte

Let us adjourn for a Tall Iced De-Caffeinated Latte
until our sly mouths are masked with froth
as though in a Noh Play or Comedia Del Arte.

Exhausted by love or travel yet never having enough
we need to pause, to pause and then relate
our various stories - be they parable or bluff-

over a Tall Iced De-Caffeinated Latte.
Inside we are stalking the secret parts of each other,
either to lower expectation or to up the ante

with a shy bravura or a rough
timidity, unsure enough to parade a cinema verite
version of ourselves in which we must believe

as the overworked waitress - tired, impatient, catty -
sighs all the way through our hors d'oeuvres,
our salmon-mousse, our liver pate, our Maron Glacé, all the way
                  through to this Tall Iced De-Caffeinated Latte

which is where the moment tightens like a nerve
staring at each other over an empty plate
both too cool or too reserved to give

an opening to the other. To declare ourselves the interested party.
Instead we wipe the coffee-froth from off each others mouths
as if in a Noh Play or Comedia Del Arte

to lower expectation or to call a bluff
behind the shade of a Tall Iced De-Caffeinated Latte.
Maybe our mouths remember the needle-tinge of Angastoura Bitters
                        in Vermouth

enough to make us furtively fence and hesitate?
Yet surely we deserve to get what we deserve
sipping on separate straws at our Tall Iced De-Caffeinated Latte?

King Size Rizlas

Apparently, the high-caste dandy, arm enlivened by an octoroon
plots to take a taper to Arcady.
Her black-purple nipples are medallions
struck by the spell of a Petrus Borel or a Philothee O'Neddy.

His elegant verse sees nothing perverse in *Les Lesbiennes*.
He lives in *The Painter's Studio* by Courbet.
A milk-swirl of syphilis spirochetes are searing his mien.
His taste astringent as a lemon sorbet.

He observes the dirt on his shirt-cuffs
with as much care as he fashions the turn of a sonnet.
Miss Lemur or Miss Prosper plucks a sheaf

from the slush-pile of *Les Fleurs Du Mal* to light up a spliff.
Her ankle rests on a cushion painted by Manet.
Her mind on the coa-coa palms and the roiling surf.

Barbary Ape

As it happens, the critic or connosieur
straining his eyes to a blur
at this Rousseau painting [he wants the message delivered
knowing Rousseau has been a postman] perceives 'the exotic' as being
    embodied
by this sly figure of the Barbary Ape,
-this ape that might well make
a furry epaulette for some pirate or cling
to the tenuous link of a creeper and swing
across this overly-luscious landscape. Nitpicking.
Both the ape and the connosieur are nitpicking.
It's so hot here a premature plum falling from its tree has ripened
before it can hit the ground.
A panting jaguar stalks the critic
at the edge of his mind. Also a duck and her drake in neon-orange
    anoraks
trail their silvery tines of light behind them as they rake
the waters in which the critic or connosieur is trailing in their wake.
Meanwhile shafts of late sunlight refracted beneath a low palm's
    underhang
translates a gnat into nothing
to show the connossieur that he is wrong.
For him 'beauty' is 'economy', spiriting or pirating
away its very essence, filling up his coffers
on some sojourn to The Gulf or to The Cape. [Any offers?
No reaction.] There's certainly no denying the many who demand
something as corny and clear as a tear calcifying into a diamond
that we must drop directly in their hand. And yet we must deny them,
deny them the comfort of any such obvious theme
much as if the jaguar inside the critic's mind had eaten him up to the
    hock.

We must shipwreck
the critic on this tiny island
that hides behind another wider island.
He must live on the thin
pulp of making, on locusts and ennui,
make firm friends with a palm-frond. Catalogue the sand.
Catch a flying-fish. Gut it. Let it live or die by his own hand.
Or wish. As we're really nitpicking now -let's strand him entirely
                              alone in this desperately-lush landscape
with nothing but a quarter-moon of melon-rind and a Barbary ape.

St Elsewhere

1] Singing Halfway To Paradise And Only Half Meaning It

Sirre, where we're living now is Relative Obscurity, that is
                               Relative Obscurity
New Mexico, where the mesquite-spring
is down to a droplet or else merely a mirage. There's a *Long-*
                               Island Iced Tea
on the verandah-rail and a respite from things

[overhead
a single humming-bird headed for Baton Rouge on only one wing
is overheard
squawking 'debtors, flies and dust all settle. I won't settle for
                               anything']

the scrape and torque of it all. Sirre, where we're headed is Elsewhere,
a city of some promise -though
the map-maker had a migraine

that day and missed it off completely. We'll get there or else
maybe halfway would do. Here's a *Poloroid* of us, here
now. Two specks of grain in a granary.

2] The Castaway

Supposedly, its been rumoured
that the boulder
that blocked the Nazarene's tomb has been whittle
-ed down by time, wind and wave to the size of an avacado or
                               peach

-stone. Word has it that its somewhere on this beach
amongst umpteen billions of other stones
scattered beneath these half-buried roots of firs
or maybe Cedars of Lebanon.

As you try to settle on the narrow strip of your flimsy beach-towel
with an airport novel
-*Who's your favourite Spice-girl?*

Mary Magdelene'-
you wonder, perhaps, if its not the very same one
now nagging insistently underneath your shoulder.

3] Our Lady Of Guadaluope

Jerome K Jerome
sat on an auburn top-knot;
the entire oeuvre of Pliny The Elder
on crow-black curlicues; John Steinbeck plonked on a tom-boy crop-

then Brecht, Bataille and Baudelaire balancing on
the beehives, moused perms, bangs and braids-
for truely, 2.30 Sunday afternoon, was where one learnt what
                art meant
recalls the fickle Consul [for it is writ and has been said

The Platonic Ideal of the ultimate
tome is always floating inches above your head]
concealed as he is, drenched in the salt-flecked yuccas, breathing in

the purr, the sigh of the ocean
as The Young Girls Of Our Lady Of Guadaluope
sashay out for their lesson in deportment.

Big Sur

Instantaneously, the sound of a blood-orange being peeled came
                        to my ear,
then the sound of its scent releasing. Henry Miller playing a
                        nude at ping-pong. Hieronymous Bosch.
The death-rattle of sleek stones in the wave-wash.
A paperback splayed like a seabird. I've never been there.

Indolent Beach Bum

'Paradise, like Bohemia, has no coast'
William Empson

As they describe it, the surf seemed like froth on a wild magnolia,
    whole rolls of it, incoming, under the salt-tang sunshine.
They say he's come to repair the ache in his liver
    with a head full of Hegel and all his ghosts on-line.

That crazy salt-lines vein the lazy beach,
    exclusive realm of the indolent, supine beach bum,
an etiolated starfish on the dateline. See Hegel and his ghosts broach
    the egg-shell skin of his cerebellum.

Gently. Doing nothing was absolutely what he once did best
    but he'd forgotten. The surf reminds him.
He needs emptiness badly, emptiness and rest
    with a punishing Id and Ego to becalm. [Subdue? Becalm]

Now that The Young Hegelians have long since put to sea
    his sly eyes are shaded by a long, elegant arm.
Maybe his own. Maybe a certain someone. Sea
    -mist is caught on the spiky tips of the ilex tree, on magnolia-
        balm,

whose heady aroma and influence has fallen upon our shy,
    indolent beach bum as the knowledge of sweetness and loss
humbles and defrocks him, comes in waves and recedes equally.
    He wears a fine peacock-feather in his hatband and though
        without redress,

knows the exact circumference of each stone. He's a dilletante
of sand. He has halved his needs as one
might halve a peach or avocado, though now he concentrates
upon a single stone, -extant-
or upon the hollow it leaves behind [By the way his *Sony-
Walkman* is tuned

to Chick Corea, Herbie Hancock and two duelling pianos,
running in rehearsal through -*In The Mood, Mood Indigo,
I'm In The Mood For Love* with a well-
drilled band
and several other such tunes]
as he rolls a cigarillo or quaffs Agua Sin Gas with his one,
free hand

as his ears warm to a particular tough
-tricksy solo or his fingers tap to *The Dry Cleaner From Des
Moines* by Charlie Mingus
[arranged by Joni Mitchell from the LP *Mingus*] on a rough-
hewn drum. Here, even the pine-needles re-arrange
themselves for him, for us

shoaling east like filings under his feet. He knows from non-
Euclidian
Geometry that two parallel lines eventually meet and find
accord.
He knows that a flock, - if you can call them a flock - of photons
flooding through a slit in cardboard

[like the deft canvas-slit of a work by Fontana] leave behind
not only a pattern of the route they appear
to have taken but also the other route they had in mind
to take but then declined. But now all such froth, such foam,
such sheer

affrontery, is receding in our low-rent, indolent beach bum
    who once contained so much of this stuff that
he would snuff out a truth if he stum
        -bled anywhere near it. Now he could email the Large Cloud
            Of Margellan. Now he's closer in spirit

to an avocado stone, to wave-froth, scree,
    to pumice or obsidian as he bare
-ly fills the sailcloth hammock slung between two trees
    that bend and shadow over him like parents bend and shadow
        over

a cot. Anyhow, this is where we leave him, and also, maybe, her -
    as the surf comes in like that haunting motif
from Nina Simone's reading of *My Father's*
    Eyes [written by Carole King] -Track 1, Side 4, of her late
        classic *Baltimore*

or *Hey, Girl, Don't Bother Me* by The Drifters or The Tams- our sly,
    indolent, utterly empty beach bum
    and his significant other. See, they've just dived
into the on-coming froth of a wild magnolia. There, no, wait, there.
    Is it them?
Mr Flotsam and Ms Jetsam- if anyone from here's to be believed.

Acupuncture

Waking, needle-sharp and aching in the clearing,
naked beneath the pines
they began to recover the bits of themselves they had lost

making love the previous evening
when their loud moans and the pine-moans
melded and their veins ran with pine-sap and pine-zest.

Now that the low-level cloud is dispersing
and a held raindrop is tense as a xylophone
or wind-chime waiting for sound, they simultaneously sense the
                start of a quest.

They suddenly know that theramin of the mind- a high wind
                singing
through pines. They know the pine-cone's
intricate complications. They even know that 'bon-san' might
                mean 'priest'.

They know about the impurities of idle living
and the sixteen zones
of being. They recommend their therapist to go and see a
                therapist

-a therapist of pines. There are fumaroles and geysers and the
                inkling
of a ground-tremor in their bones.
Pine-bark and pine-gum are sweet and sharp to their taste.

They know the sky is the absolute blue of a painting
by Yves Klein,
that is, Yves Klein Blue No 2, against which their white bodies
           recently wrest

-led. They know that the taste of each other is the tang
of pine-resin and that a low foen, supine,
is moving in around the bare knees of their pine forest.

They know all this without thinking,
pricked into life, pricked into being, emblazoned,
their backs stinging with hundred of tiny needles shoaling east.